JEWEL STICKER STORIES
TREASURE HUNT!

By Catherine Daly-Weir
Illustrated by Cathy Beylon

Grosset & Dunlap • New York

Copyright © 1998 by Grosset & Dunlap, Inc. Illustrations copyright © 1998 by Cathy Beylon. All rights reserved.
Published by Grosset & Dunlap, Inc., a member of Penguin Putnam Books for Young Readers, New York.
GROSSET & DUNLAP is a trademark of Grosset & Dunlap, Inc. Published simultaneously in Canada.
Printed in the U.S.A.
ISBN 0-448-41848-7   B C D E F G H I J

Captain Bob was a pirate. But he wasn't a very good one.

Sure he had an eye patch, a parrot named Polly, and he said "Yo-ho-ho" a lot. But there was just one problem.

"Shiver me timbers," he said to Polly. "I have never found me a treasure."

It made Captain Bob very sad.

Captain Bob may not have a treasure, but he does have a gold watch! Can you find it and put a jewel sticker on it?

Early the next morning, Captain Bob's trusty first mate, Annie, pounded on his door. "Captain Bob!" she shouted. "Wake up! We found a message in a bottle!"

Captain Bob opened the door. "Ahoy there, matey," he said. "I'll be right there."

Captain Bob has lots of sea treasures in his room. Do you see a sand dollar? Put a jewel sticker on it.

Captain Bob quickly got dressed and ran on deck. The entire crew was waiting. What was in the bottle?

Captain Bob removed the cork and pulled out the message. He put on his glasses and read the note:

> *You want to find treasure? Fancy that!*
> *Start by looking underneath your pirate* _____.

Captain Bob scratched his head. He pulled his beard. "I do want to find treasure! But I'm not sure what this means," he said.

"Is it Siamese cat?" Captain Bob looked underneath his cat, Felix. Nothing.

"Is it baseball bat? Or maybe spoiled brat?" he wondered.

Do you know where Captain Bob should look? If you do, put a sticker on it!

"Hat," said Polly.

"Oh, I got it!" said Captain Bob. "Maybe it's underneath my hat!"

Polly sighed.

Captain Bob took off his pirate hat. And there, in the lining, was a treasure map!

"Well, blow me down!" said Captain Bob. "This map leads to an island in the middle of the ocean!"

So they raised the anchor and off they sailed.

Do you see Captain Bob's kitten, Felix?
Put a jewel sticker on his collar.

Captain Bob looked around. The sea was empty and still.

"What do I do now?" asked Captain Bob.

Just then a passing sea gull dropped a bottle right on Captain Bob's head!

"Ouch!" said Captain Bob. "That hurt!"

He picked up the bottle and was just about to throw it overboard.

"Stop! Message!" squawked Polly.

"Shiver me timbers," said Captain Bob. "There's a message inside!" He unrolled it and read:

> *You'll find treasure, to your relief,*
> *hidden in the coral _____.*

"Oh, my," said Captain Bob. "This is a toughie. Could it be beef? Or leaf? Or maybe grief?"

Can you find the member of the crew wearing a yellow shirt and blue boots? Give that pirate a jewel sticker to wear!

You'll find treasure, to your relief, hidden in the coral ____.

Polly rolled her eyes. "Reef," she said.

"Eureka! You're right!" cried Captain Bob. "I'm going to put on my bathing trunks right now!"

A minute later, Captain Bob held his nose and jumped overboard.

He swam down, down, down until he got to the beautiful coral reef. There were pretty fish, lots of sea horses, and a big octopus.

See the friendly mermaid pointing to the clue? Why don't you put a jewel sticker in her hair?

Now that you've already taken a dip, Why don't you head to the sunken _____?

With the mermaid's help, Captain Bob found the clue and came back up for air. The captain read the note out loud while the fish nibbled on his toes:

> Now that you've already taken a dip,
> Why don't you head to the sunken _____?

Captain Bob thought long and hard.
"I know!" he finally said. "Potato chip!"
Polly rolled her eyes.
"Trip? Slip?" he suggested.
"Sunken ship!" Polly squawked.
"Sunken ship!" said Captain Bob. "But how do I find it?"
Just then a friendly dolphin popped out of the water. He scooped up Captain Bob and took him for a ride! The ship followed close behind.

Look at all the colorful fish. Put a jewel sticker on your favorite one.

"Whee!" cried Captain Bob as the dolphin jumped through the waves. "This is fun!"
Finally they came to a stop.
"Is this where the sunken ship is?" asked Captain Bob.
The dolphin nodded, then dove underwater.
Yes! There was a spooky old sunken ship.

Do you see the message?
Put a jewel sticker on it so
Captain Bob can find it too!

Thanks to you, Captain Bob found the next message. He climbed back on board his ship, waved good-bye to the dolphin, and read the next clue:

>The treasure is within your reach!
>Just head on over to your favorite pink sand _____.

The crew looked puzzled.

"Hmmm," said Captain Bob. "Is it bloodsucking leech? Fuzzy peach?"

"Beach!" squawked Polly.

"That's it! Beach!" said Captain Bob happily. "And my favorite pink sand beach is on Skull Island! All hands on deck! Full speed ahead. Next stop, Skull Island!"

The treasure is within your reach! Just head on over to your favorite pink sand ——.

Do you see Skull Island?
Mark it with a jewel sticker.

Take ten
eps forward
nd close your
yes. Count
o 100 for a big
surprise!

Captain Bob jumped off the ship and ran onto the beautiful pink sand beach. And there, taped to a palm tree, was another clue. Captain Bob read it out loud to Polly:

> *Take ten steps forward and close your eyes.*
> *Count to 100 for a big surprise!*

Captain Bob took ten steps forward and closed his eyes. Then he slowly counted to 100. Nothing happened.

"This is silly," he said to Polly. "When can I open my eyes?"

"Open your eyes!" squawked Polly.

So Captain Bob did.

**Do you see a little crab peeking
his head out of his hole in the sand?
Mark it with a jewel sticker.**

"SURPRISE! Happy Birthday, Captain Bob!"

It was a big party, with all of Captain Bob's friends. The dolphin, the mermaid, and even the sea gull were all there to celebrate.

"Oh, thank you!" said Captain Bob. "Friends are the best treasure of all!"

Make the lanterns glow
with your jewel stickers.

That's when Captain Bob spotted his birthday gift—a pirate's treasure!

"But gold doubloons and pieces of eight aren't too bad either!" he said.

Decorate Captain Bob's birthday treasure with the rest of your jewel stickers!